C000136089

LUNA GLOBAL MEDIA

Suncrest Dv. Melbourne, FL

+1 321 234 7030 U.S.

https://lunaglobalmedia.com/

GHOSTLY TALES AND CURIOUS STORIES FROM ENGLAND

ISBN (Paperback): 979-8-9888550-9-5

Printed in the United States of America

GHOSTLY TALES AND CURIOUS STORIES FROM ENGLAND

BY

ANNA RAINS

TABLE OF CONTENTS

THE ELIZABETHAN FARMHOUSE
A haunted house

Jenny called her husband excitedly. 'Hi Rob. You know the old house that I have always loved? It has come on to the market and is up for auction in two weeks' time. Can we go and see it – Please?'

'Hold on a minute' her cautious husband replied, 'you're not thinking of us buying it are you?'

'Well maybe - maybe not. I just want to go and look inside. I've made an appointment for this weekend. The kids can come too.'

'But it's been empty for at least forty years. It must be in a terrible state.'

'Thank you. 2:30pm on Saturday afternoon.'

'As long as it won't take too long – I want to watch the rugby.'

And that's how it all started.

The old man who owned it had moved into the small cottage alongside and had just left the big half-timbered farmhouse dating back to Tudor days.

Ivy and Virginia creeper almost covered it. Walls, roof and chimneys, so it was hard to really tell what it was like.

He had died intestate and it had taken a long time to sort everything out. Another ten years of neglect perhaps.

There had been a number of relatives scattered all over the place, including Australia and so the solicitors had a tough time contacting everyone. Finally, it had come down to the sale of a building once admired and appreciated by everyone in the village and surrounding areas. Many local people referred to the house as The Manor and that was what it became known as – The Manor of Little Mottram.

Jenny didn't tell her husband that she had already requested the buyers pack so that she knew how much they would have to put down if they purchased it.

It was a bit daunting to enter the side door. The front one was warped and wouldn't budge. The side one led into the old back kitchen – complete with a sink that must have been hundreds of years old and a massive iron fireplace, above which washing had been suspended in far off days.

Cobwebs covered in dust hung from the old shelves and ceilings, although the estate agent had managed to sweep away some of them to allow visitors to pass through without getting their hair full of the disgusting grey strands which swooped down towards the floor. Rob was tall and so crowned himself with a halo of ancient ragged, black dust and dirt filled swathes.

On one side the pantry still contained pottery and stone jugs and vases. Jars that had been left, containing whatever a careful wife or maid had filled them with.

Now solid mould was all that was inside the glass containers.

Henry, usually known as Harry, their eldest son, tripped over an old iron doorstop half hidden by overgrown shrubs and plants, in his eagerness to get inside. His sister, Lou held back, while Jenny carried the eighteen-month-old Jake.

An old iron mangle, its rubber rollers long perished propped up the stable door leading into the kitchen. More devastation.   Piles of ancient newspapers lay beside the fire ready to be used to start the old black kitchen stove, part cooker, with its iron doored bread oven. All looked so forlorn and unloved.

Rob looked around and quailed at the thought of all the work to be done – let alone any restoration the old house needed.

Jenny darted from room to room imagining the house as she would make it. Christmas in front of a great roaring fire in the drawing room. Dining room restored and painted with a warm red, candles down the centre of a big table, decorations everywhere. She had mentally moved in!

She vaguely wondered if it had a ghost but Jenny was too outgoing to bother to think much about it. No ghost was going to disturb her! That was where she was so wrong. But it would be a long time before the full force of evil spirits crossed their paths.

Theirs was almost the only bid at the auction. One other person began but dropped out very quickly. Jenny said, 'Where's the champagne?' While Rob wanted to drown his sorrows in a bottle of whisky.

It was theirs and they were able to wander and look as much as they wanted.

'Mum, there's a cellar down here, can we go and look?'

'No not without your father.'

'Dad, there's a locked door, I think it leads up to the attic! Can we go up? Asked Harry enthusiastically, 'I bet there's some treasure up there!'

'No' replied his father. 'The floor boards might be rotten.' Which they probably were given the loose stone slabs on the roof.

They decided to sort the little cottage out for them to live in while they began the mammoth task of bringing the old house back to life.

Huge skips were ordered to clear both cottage and farmhouse – and the outbuildings, old stables and cowsheds, which they hadn't really noticed. Maybe the children can have a pony later, mused Jenny. There was plenty of land and the paddock behind the house looked as though it may have been used for horses or cattle before.

The children discovered an old hay barn with a rickety looking wooden ladder and were eager to go and explore, but their father was quite firm again.

'No, not until I've had time to check it out myself.'

The old man had been a hoarder, but where Rob just wanted to throw everything into the skips, Jenny told him she wanted to check it all out in case there was anything worth keeping. An old tin trunk was one of the items discovered.

'I am sure there is something in it' said Jenny, as she shook it and got a reassuring sound. She wasn't satisfied until Rob forced the catch. Nothing exciting was found inside. Just some old tools and rusty nails and bits and pieces no-one knew what they been used for. No deeds or ancient papers or maps or other treasures had been hidden inside. Rob was ready to throw it all into the nearest skip. But Jenny wouldn't allow him to.

They began at the back door. Clearing and cleaning as they went. Some things Jenny put on one side, but mostly Rob got his way.

The back kitchen was quite a large room, something they hadn't appreciated when it was so full of discarded junk.

'Fantastic place for our wellies and outdoor coats and things and great for the dog to sleep.'

'But we haven't got a dog' muttered Rob knowing he was wasting his breath.

'No not yet,' replied Jenny, 'but I've always thought it is good for the kids to grow up with animals.

Gradually they moved further into the house. Layers of old wallpaper hung they're by previous owners were peeling off.

In the kitchen they threw out the old stove and installed an AGA, while painting the walls a cheerful yellow.

No problems here. It was as if the old house was giving its approval.

Rob got some local men in to help clear generations of overgrown shrubs and trees. Ladders were put up against the walls and the ivy and Virginia creeper pulled away, exposing the windows with small diamond shaped panes of glass. Many of the windows had missing panes and others were going to need to be completely renewed. It would take a long time, but Rob just shrugged and reminded himself they were planning to live here for a long time.

While he was outside, Jenny moved into the drawing room. A room she loved. Low dark beams, light splashing through the windows and on to spring flowers she had arranged in vases. A big mirror was mounted above the enormous open fireplace. She had joked that they could cook an ox on there – no trouble at all! She arranged the comfortable sofas and chairs and placed the few bits of furniture they had against the walls.

Some pictures and some lovely bright furnishings, in keeping with the style of the house, would make it perfect.

By this time, they had moved in. Each child had his or her own bedroom – not yet fully furnished – but you couldn't do everything at once, she reminded herself. The bedroom she and Rob shared was looking straight, if not exactly the way she was planning.

The big playroom on the first floor with its lovely large windows looking out over the front garden, faced south. It had such a nice feel to it. She smiled as she thought about this room, filled with their toys and games. Although, Harry liked to use his electronic games in the quiet of his own room, she could imagine the children playing happily together in there.

Later, she dated the beginning of the unrest to the time when she began on the dining room.

It began almost imperceptibly. Odd little things. There had been the occasion of the vase of flowers she had arranged and placed on the window sill in the drawing room. Jenny, after she'd seen Rob off to work and taken Henry and Lou just up the road to the village primary school, and Jake to nursery she decided to get on while everything was peaceful

I'll go and clean out the hearth and lay the fire for this evening, she said to herself. They had friends coming over and she wanted everything to be nice. As she walked into the drawing room Jenny noticed a flower was lying beside the vase and not in it.

Odd, she thought. I only put those in there an hour ago. She placed the flower back in the water and left the room to fetch some kindling, returned and noticed the same flower was out again. This time she shook her head. I am sure I replaced it. Still, as she was busy, she soon forgot about it.

Then a few days later she noticed a cushion on one of the big armchairs near the fire. She had 'fluffed' all the cushions that morning and now one of them looked as though someone had been sitting on it and squashed it down. Shaking her head, she fluffed it up again. What was going on? Was she going mad?

She didn't say anything to Rob. He was busy enough without her filling his head with things that were probably just her imagination.

She went back to the dining room. Funny how it always felt cold, even though it faced south. She was determined to get more of the old and tired flock paper off the walls. Part of it was hanging listlessly anyway.

Was it her imagination that made her feel she was being watched?

Using a heated wallpaper stripper and lots of dissolving gunk, she tackled the bit round the fireplace. Suddenly a huge lump of soot fell into the black hole where long-gone fires had burned brightly. She jumped. Did she hear someone cackling with laughter? No, don't be silly, she told herself out loud. Get on with it!

Pulling more of the thick red paper away, someone's pride and joy, she found more paper below. Also red. I am working along the same lines as those who had gone before me. I had always seen this room as red – she continued to murmur to herself.

An hour more as the pile of filthy wallpaper had grown round her feet, before she had to leave to collect Jake from nursery. Jenny had turned Abba on as background music. 'Waterloo' blared out. She loved the bright and cheerful music – although she knew it wasn't Rob's taste. I'll leave it on, she said out loud, after making herself a little less like a homeless tramp.

Jake was chatty as they walked home holding hands. But as they stepped in through the back door, Jenny was shocked to hear, not Abba, but some dreadful, almost macabre, music coming from the dining room. She quickly rushed in and silenced it. What was that? I would never play music, if you could call it music, like that?

Shaking, she asked Jake what he would like for lunch, although she knew he would opt for fish fingers and chips. Mechanically, she prepared his lunch, still wondering how the music had changed. Who had switched the programme?

She settled Jake down on a sofa to watch his favourite CBB's channel, knowing he would probably doze off, and forced herself back into the dining room. Contrary to her fears, she had an uneventful afternoon.

After collecting Harry and Lou from school and listening to their chatter, she suddenly noticed that Jake had disappeared.

'Where's Jake' she asked the other children.

'Probably in the playroom with his friends', remarked Lou in a disinterested voice.

'What do you mean, his friends?' By this time Jenny was close to panicking.

'His imaginary friends' replied Harry, as though this was a normal thing.

Jenny rushed up the wide oak staircase. She stopped outside the playroom door. Was that children's laughter she heard? Then Jake was responding. There aren't any other children here! What is happening?

She slipped into the room and listened. Nothing. She quietly asked Jake who he had been talking to.

'My friend Charles. Mum, can he have tea with us tonight?' She hated that word, but supposed the children were going to copy their friends.

'Of course, darling. What would he like to eat?' She felt like a fool, but Jake didn't seem to notice.

'Same as us.

Downstairs in the big kitchen she laid out knives and forks and glasses. Jake quickly reminded her that Charles was joining them and she hadn't laid a place for him. She quietly did as she was told. Now, I am going mad, she thought – laying a place for a ghost! There she'd said it – a ghost.

'Mummy, Charles likes the playroom. He says it used to be his playroom, but some bad men came and knocked down a lot of things. Bad men stayed in his playroom and he wasn't allowed to go in there. It made him very unhappy. He's happy now because he likes being in there'.

'Does he darling? Tell him I am so pleased'.

Oh God! Now I am talking to my son's imaginary friend! I must be going mad!

She had planned to do some more work in the dining room that evening, but couldn't bear to work in there when it was dark outside. Instead, she gave the children baths, read them a story and tucked them into their own beds. 'Nite, nite she called out as she headed downstairs again.

At the bottom of the stairs, she shied away from the dining room door. There were shadows everywhere. Dark corners that made her decide they needed better lighting. I must ask Rob to get an electrician here as soon as possible. For now, she went round and turned on every light she could find. Blow the electricity bills, she told herself.

Was she scared? Yes, she told herself. What is there about this house? It's only bricks and mortar!

Later in bed, Rob said, 'By the way Jen, I don't think I told you but when we were clearing the growth on the outside, we found what looked like bricked up church windows. They were arched and not like anything else in the house'.

Anything is possible in this horrible house she thought.

Next morning as if to confirm, she'd gone into the dining room and found the fireirons laid out in the shape of a cross – facing east. She snatched them up and put them back by the fire hearth.

'Rob, where are you?'

'I'm here' he called back'.

'Rob, you know the very old wooden cross we found lying amongst the rubbish in the dining room? What did we do with it? We didn't throw it out, did we?'

'No, it's somewhere out in one of the stables – I'll look for it this weekend'.

'No, go and find it now!' Her voice sounded a little hysterical.

'Be reasonable, Jen, I'm off to cut the grass, I'll get it later'.

'Now – please' she almost begged.

While he left to do as asked, Jenny found two tall candle sticks, the kind you see in churches. She placed them on either side of the hearth. I'll move the mirror from above the fireplace and hang the cross there. The altar must have been about here, she said out loud. I wonder when they built the fireplace. It had obviously been installed much later than the walls surrounding it.

She dashed round to the outside wall, and found as Rob said, the arched shape of the windows. I'll tell Rob to get the builders in as soon as possible to remove the stones and open up the spaces. They would have been either side of where the altar must have been she decided. If I restore the old chapel perhaps the ghosts might leave us alone!

After that things calmed down and she was allowed to work on the dining room in peace.

'It's all OK', she told Rob. That was until they uncovered the priest hole – then things got really nasty!

Some weeks later, Rob was heading down the wide, oak staircase. 'Jenny what were you doing in the attic?

'I wasn't in the attic'.

'Yes, you were, I saw you coming down the stairs leading from it.'

Jenny looked at him. Looked straight in to his eyes, 'Believe me Rob, I haven't been upstairs all morning. Perhaps you are catching the farmhouse fever!'

'No, I'm not. You were wearing that long old housecoat you used to live in before Jake was born'.

'But I threw that out years ago – before we moved in here'.

Rob looked confused but just let it go.

The following weekend, they decided to take down the old velvet curtain hanging on the wall near the spare room. It was very old and tired and faded in places where the sun had shone through the landing windows.

There was nothing behind it, just a bricked up and then plastered wall. That's strange they both thought. Why would anyone hang a curtain there? That was until they saw the faint marks of what had been a doorway.

'There is something behind there, I'm sure,' said Rob. 'I'm going to get my sledge hammer and have a go at it.'

'No, please leave it Rob, I'm getting horrible vibes.

But undeterred, Rob found his tools and began to hack away at what had been the door frame. The walls were quite thick and so progress was slow. He managed to clear a small hole through which he could see, when he shone a torch in, appeared to be a tiny room.

'I wonder what it was for and why it was bricked up' Jenny didn't answer. There had been too many strange things about this house, she didn't dare to speculate on something else.

It took several days, and a lot of hard work, to open up the entrance. Inside was a room about six feet square. In the corner they found stairs leading down to the kitchen chimney.

'Do you think it was a priest hole? Asked Rob.

'It can be anything it likes. Just brick it up again.' Jenny shrieked.

'Do you know what is odd, Jen? The air smells quite fresh and there are no cobwebs or dust in here, and when I touched the old candle on that little table by the wall, it was warm as though someone had just blown it out.

That was enough for Jenny. 'That does it Rob. I'm taking myself and the children to my mother's house and we are not coming back until someone has come in and exorcised it!

But that night the old house had one last violent fling at them. They were all in the sitting room watching an old film.

Suddenly there was one hell of a crash in the dining room. Everybody looked at each other. What was that? Rob was the only one brave enough to go and look.

'It's that mirror, Jen. The one you propped up against the wall. It has fallen on its face and the glass is completely smashed'.

'How did it do that? Jenny almost whispered. 'It was leaning at an angle with its back to the wall. Either someone pushed it over, or it miraculously jumped up and fell forwards.

All of them were now very afraid. At that moment, all the electricity in the house went off. Everything was black.

'Rob, can you feel your way over to the fireplace? There is a candle lighter and candles there. We need to light as many of them as we can'.

'Mum, I'm really scared' wailed Lou.

'So am I' said Harry'.

Jake just burst into wild and loud sobbing.

Rob went round lighting as many candles as he could find. They helped, but the shadows grew darker and more sinister. Candles flickered for no reason. One or two went out as though someone had extinguished them.

'That's it. I am taking the children and going to my mother's tomorrow morning. Whoever they are have been trying to get us to leave. Well, they've won'.

They crept upstairs to bed together. Rob collected the children's bedding and brought it into their bedroom.

None of them slept well that night. Strange groaning noises seem to spring from the ancient timbers. Wind howled round the house as if trying to find a way in. Early next morning they packed their bags.

As they left, Jenny said to Rob, 'I'm not coming back until someone from the church has been here to clear all the evil out.

That night, where the arched windows had been, colours of lights emanated as if the stained glass had somehow been restored; inside the former church a flickering light moved around the space, as if a person or persons paced up and down restlessly, waiting for the return of the woman who had brought them back from the dead...

BEHIND CLOED DOORS
Or behind the forbidden curtain.

She had dressed so carefully for her nephew's wedding. Everything had to be perfect – hair, makeup and her outfit. Did she look older? Yes of course she did. It had been nearly twenty-five years since they'd last met. What would he think? What will I think of him?

Emily had known him since she was fifteen when she began crewing for him in his racing dinghy. She thought she had fallen in love from the very beginning – knowing he'd always thought of her as the teenage sister of her brother Christopher, who was to become his best friend and so she knew Will and his wife Jane were bound to be at the wedding.

Emily was feeling very anxious and almost snapped at her husband for not getting ready in time.

"What's the rush" he'd asked.

"You know I hate being late Jack"

"Yes, but we've got plenty of time to get to the church, so just calm down a bit". Her husband didn't know of the tensions building up inside of her.

The wedding was fine. She had noticed Will in a pew behind where the family were assigned to sit. The smile he gave her made her heart turn over. Don't be such a fool, she told herself. Look at

15

his wife, dressed in a very elegant outfit and Emily felt a bit dowdy. I shouldn't have chosen such a bright blue, she said to herself.

Champagne and photographs over, they all made their way into the hall where the elegant tables were laid out. She glanced at the table plan and was so happy to find Bill and his wife were on the same table.

Emily found the four of them were sitting together with Bill right beside her. I wonder if that was Chris's idea?

She smiled with happiness. It had been such a long time since her brother's special birthday and the last time she'd met Will.

They began swopping memories and names of people they had known, gradually rekindling their interests in each other, while they accepted more champagne.

"I always cared for you" she found herself almost whispering to Will.

"Why didn't you tell me? I thought it was Jamie you were keen on and so I backed off".

"No, it was always you".

"How stupid I was".

The wine flowed and so did their conversation, each of them revealing more of their feelings. It was when they danced together and she seemed to melt into his arms that she felt the same longing and desire fill her body and she knew she was still in love with him.

His hand found her knee and he was gently caressing it making her almost lost in her dreams.

Her husband announced he was going to bed. "Don't rush, you have so many memories and stories to reminisce about".

Will's wife disappeared shortly after.

"Come on, this old house is fascinating. Let's go and explore".

Taking his hand she happily rose to her feet. Both of them knowing there would be no holding back this time.

Giggling now after too many glasses of champagne, they found a long corridor with a curtain from another age and a rope across guarding an entrance.

'Private, do not enter', said a sign hanging from the rope. Ignoring it they pulled it aside and crept forward causing the wooden floorboards to creak, as if to emphasise they were not welcome. Part way along a single light hung from the ceiling causing strange shadows to slide out from an ancient fireplace. Emily held Will's hand even tighter and said she was scared, perhaps they had better go back, but now Will was insisting. He told her he'd been stupid in the past, but this time he wanted to find out what he'd missed. She giggled at this and willingly moved forward beside him, glancing into old and tired bedrooms and dressing rooms.

That was until they found the 'room'! It was as if it had its own illumination. In the centre of the room stood a magnificent four poster bed. Bright tapestry curtains hung from the heavy wooden framework. A cover was drawn over the made-up bed – everything ready for the two of them, Will thought.

Pictures of former men and women were seen in gold covered frames hung on oak panelled walls.

Will led Emily into the bedroom. Inside he took her into his arms and began kissing her. At first lightly before both of them kissed each other with all the longing and desire built up over years of waiting.

Emily shuddered. "It's cold in here" she murmured through their kisses.

Will pointed to the bed. "Come on, I'll warm you up". As he said that, he noticed the door into the room slowly closing behind them, as if an unseen hand was quietly shutting it. He frowned slightly but was so eager to make love to this woman he had known since they were teenagers.

Emily allowed him to lead her towards the great ornate bed. Before they reached it the lights vanished and they found themselves standing in pitch darkness.

"What the hell!" Will said.

Emily just held on tighter.

"Let's go. I'm scared!"

"So am I" confessed Will. "I've got my phone with me. It's got a torch on it. Hang on a minute while I get it out." He switched it on. The light flickered for a second and faded. They were in pitch darkness again. There hadn't been time for them to work out where they, or the door was.

Emily was close to fainting.

"Look, you just stand here while I feel around for the door".

"No, I'm not letting go of you", panic in her voice.

"I think it must be over there. We just came straight in".

Both of them reached out with their arms, stretching them out in every direction in the hopes of finding the door.

Emily caught something. It felt like the hanging drapes of the four-poster bed. For a moment she hung on, and then, as if this triggered what happened next, they heard the sound of crashing timbers behind them and guessed the ancient bed had collapsed. At that moment there was frantic mewing and screeching of a cat and the air filled with the smell of ancient rotten dust and dirt, almost chocking them.

Now thoroughly terrified they were even more desperate to escape.

Will's hand felt a round knob and he prayed this was the door and not a cupboard. At that moment he thought he'd felt something clawing at his face. Forcing the door open, the dim light in the corridor felt like a huge crystal chandelier had been turned on.

Half dragging Emily now, they began to stumble and run away from that dreadful room. Will couldn't help glancing back over his shoulder only to see the door quietly closing behind them.

Later neither of them remembered how they'd found their way back to the wedding reception. By this time most people had made their way to bed except Christopher, who was still sitting near the bar, with the expression of 'thank goodness that's over'.

He looked up when he saw them come back into the room and quickly poured them a large brandy each, saying "You look as though you need this. Where the hell have you been and what happened"?

Both Emily and Will were too shocked to reply.

"What happened to your face, Will? Don't tell me Emily scratched you because you were too forward!"

Will glanced in the mirror behind Christopher and saw blood seeping from numerous deep scratches down one cheek.

"No. It must have been the cat in the four-poster room".

"What room and what cat?" Christopher asked quietly.

"We wanted to find somewhere quiet to talk", replied Will.

Christopher smiled but looked worried at the same time.

"We found a passage and decided to explore. The one behind the curtain and the sign that said 'No Entry'. Most of the place looked half derelict until we came across this room with the four-poster bed. It was lit up and seemed inviting".

Christopher said nothing and allowed Will to blurt it all out. How the lights had gone out and they'd been left in total darkness. How he'd tried to use his phone torch and that had failed. It was at this moment Will realised he'd lost his phone. He must have dropped it in their panic.

Emily just sat there as though in a semi-coma. Too stunned to add anything to the men's conversation.

Christopher began to talk. "There is an old rumour about that room. The bed has long gone. Apparently, a young couple of lovers made the same decision you were about to do. Anyway, they climbed up on to the bed and as they lay there the old bed just fell apart. The heavy beams and timbers, along with the tapestry drapes, crashed down on them, smothering and trapping them. It was several days before they were found. Everybody thought they had eloped. Nobody guessed they were still in the old house. They were found lying together on the bed under all the debris with only his hand stretched out as if appealing for help. Just inside the door a cat was discovered. Its mouth opens as though giving its last cry. Its legs and claws stretched out as if trying to claw its way out. It's said that sometimes a cat is still heard crying and scratching in that part of the house".

Neither Will nor Emily could say anything. Shock etched on both their faces.

"You go off and clean up your face William, otherwise Jane might wonder what you've been up to. Just say that you caught your cheek on the rosebush near the carpark when you went out to check on something in your car. I'll stay here with Emily. I don't think either of you should go off to join your spouses until you have recovered yourselves. You can say that the three of us sat up late talking about our teenage days.

Next day, Christopher went behind the curtain and retraced the path Will and Emily had walked. He found the room. As he expected there was nothing but dust and dirt – except Will's phone lying on the floor in the middle of the room. He picked it up and quietly returned it to its owner.

He hadn't known what to believe last night. Had they heard the story about the young couple dying in that room and were just using it to cover up their illicit liaison? But that didn't account for the deep marks of claws down one side of Will's face and neck – and how did his phone get there?

THE MONKS OF PRIEST LANE.

As she hit the brakes hard, the car slid off the loose gravel drive and ended up with its nose in the thick thorn hedge running down the side of the driveway leading to her home.

"For God's sake mum! What the hell are you doing? We nearly had a bad accident!"

"Didn't you see them?"

"See who?" asked her daughter.

"The monks. A line of them crossing the drive. They walked straight through the hedges as if they weren't there."

"No, I didn't see anything. Did you have a drink at Christine's house before you picked me up from the station?"

"No, of course I didn't. You must have seen them. A line of about fifteen walking one behind the other."

"Well, I didn't. Anyway, I was answering Jill who texted me."

"They were there. A whole line of monks dressed in dark habits. Their heads were down and so I couldn't see their faces."

"Well, where are they now? They can't have just disappeared."

"They did just vanish. That is what is so odd. They were so clear as they walked across the drive-in front of the car. They came through the hedge on my side and then through the hedge on your side."

"They couldn't have done. The hedge is too thick. Dad says he keeps it 'stock proof' so nobody could walk through its Mum. When did you last have your eyes tested?"

"Please listen to me Kate. I really did see them. Suddenly they seemed to vanish, one by one, when they were about ten feet into the field. All of them, one by one, until they had all gone".

"I'm sorry mum, it must be your eyesight."

Maggie, still shaking with the shock of it all, carefully reversed her car back on to the gravel. I'll look for damage when I get into the yard by the house, she muttered to herself.

Checking the front of the car she was relieved to find very little wrong. Not enough for her husband to query.

"Are you going to tell Dad?" asked Kate as she got out.

"No. Please Kate don't tell anyone. I've got to work this out in my head myself.

She knew what she'd seen. Nobody was going to talk her out of it – but who were they? Certainly not from this period. They had to be ghosts. A whole line of monks. Where had they gone? How could they have just walked through hedges – unless of course there weren't any there in their time? Someone, may be two hundred years ago, had lined the original cart track with hedges. These monks must have come from an earlier period.

Maggie found it hard to sleep. The images kept going through her mind. She was awake when her husband slid into bed, but she pretended to be sleeping. Next morning she got up early with an excuse she wanted to take the dog out. Slipping his collar on, she made for the gate into what she now called 'the monk's field'. Searching for

23

any evidence, she found none. Surely if they had been real people, they would have left a path in the wet grass. Nothing. No signs of the hedges on either side having been disturbed.

Puzzled and a bit confused, Maggie laid out the things for breakfast. Her husband, Brian, asked her if she was OK. She nodded her head and said nothing.

As soon as she could she began searching on google for any clues. All she found was up to date information about the old farm.

Maggie watched out of her bedroom window later but saw nothing unusual. It was on the third night after her experience she saw a light near the hedge but it also vanished in the same place the monks had disappeared.

Odd things began to happen to her. She found herself listening and sometimes taking part in some Gregorian chants that seemed to be infiltrating her head. Why? She hated that sort of churchy music she told herself. Why the chants? Did they have anything to do with the monks?

A few weeks later, Maggie had an extraordinary dream. She dreamt there was a church or chapel in the field behind the barn located on one side of the centre farmyard. It was rectangular and had stone walls four to five feet high. It was so vivid she'd taken the dog with her into this field. Nothing there – just an indentation in the field as if the ground had sunk.

What was going on? Could she have lived here five hundred years ago? Could she have in fact been one of them? Maggie believed in past lives and although anything was possible, she dismissed the idea.

Something kept drawing her back to the 'monks' field.

A friend came to visit. Maggie trusted her enough to open up about the dream, but still wasn't comfortable enough to talk about the monks. She knew Anne would accept what she had actually seen, but she told herself to see what happened in the field. Anne was also a dowser. She handed Maggie a pair of dowsing rods when they were near the dip in the dream field and the two of them walked side by side. Suddenly Maggie let out a gasp. Her rods had crossed at exactly the same moment her friend's had.

Anne confirmed there was definitely something buried there. Something quite a long way down, and no it wasn't a church or a chapel but more likely to be a hospital, or even a plague house.

"Lots of people died here. There is still so much torment coming from the earth under our feet. I am getting horror and pain and great sickness. I will try to put them at rest and release them from their terrible deaths. They are still trapped, you see", she told Maggie.

She turned to Maggie, "Why am I picking up that you were somehow involved"?

"Come and have a cup of coffee and I will tell you the rest".

The two women sat down together, and haltingly at first, Maggie opened up, telling her about her horror of nearly running over the line of monks. She explained her surprise and confusion about how they kept disappearing one by one. Her daughter hadn't seen anything and she, Maggie, hadn't told anyone, including her husband who probably would have laughed and made fun of her.

"You are the first person I've talked to about it".

Anne didn't laugh or tell her she must have been dreaming, she merely asked to be shown where it had happened. Leaving their coffee, they went through the gate into the field. Maggie showed Anne where she had seen them coming through the hedge before vanishing. They didn't stop walking, just kept on and then there was nothing, she told her friend.

Anne asked her to go and stand by the gate while she worked. She re-traced the steps the monks had taken and suddenly she stopped as though coming up against a brick wall.

After several minutes while the pendulum she was holding moved sideways and then forwards, she said, "Maggie, you can come over now. I think I understand. I stopped because I 'saw' a building in front of me with a heavy oak door. The door was closed to me because I am a stranger. I think you would have been allowed in. At this moment I don't know why. Your monks entered the doorway and disappeared from sight because they were inside a building".

Maggie stood there feeling stunned at this revelation. Then she asked, "Where is the building now?"

"Long gone. It may have been destroyed by fire. I think it was deliberately burnt down. The walls you saw at the other building were like these. I think if you dug down about three to four feet you would find them. What I would like to do is to try and work out the overall size and shape of the building".

Anne, using her dousing rods while moving around the field, putting small sticks in wherever she found a corner. After about half an hour she was satisfied. The building hadn't been rectangular but L-shaped.

Maggie asked her if it had been a church or a chapel.

"No", replied Anne. "I think the church or chapel is up there on the slope opposite, probably now hidden among the trees and shrubs surrounding that house". She pointed to a modern building half hidden by huge conifers. "You told me once that there are the remains of a Saxon Cross beside the road up there".

"Yes, there is. There's only the old stone base still there with a much later granite cross on top". It suddenly came to her – "Is this why the road is called Priest Lane? There must have been a church here at some time. The nearest is in the next village about three miles away. We can't count the little chapel further up the road because that's only been there for about one hundred years".

Anne's pendulum was swinging fiercely in circles.

"It says yes."

"Thinking back to this building. What was it and why was it here?"

"It would have been the living quarters for the monks who tended the poor souls who died in the hospital in your other field. Somewhere there would have been a place where they were buried. Any ideas?"

"There is one corner that never gets grazed. The animals don't seem to like it."

"Show me".

The two women retraced their steps past the place while Anne talked about how many people had died. They reached the corner and Anne almost reeled.

"I am not surprised", she said, "There is still a stench coming from the ground – almost like rotting bodies. That can't be because they were left here hundreds of years ago. I just don't understand. Somehow, I am still getting the feeling that you were here – that you died here".

Maggie felt drained of energy. The two women silently walked back to the house. Once there Anne asked her friend if she was willing to do some past life regression. They had to find out Maggie's connection with this place. Maggie just nodded. She needed to know. They went into Maggie's sitting room and made themselves comfortable.

"I'm not going to tell you anything. I want you to sit there and tell me what you remember".

"My name was John, after St John. We lived here. My family and I. I knew the monks and sometimes worshipped with them".

Anne just nodded.

"I'm so cold!" Maggie called out, as she began to shiver violently. Anne just sat quietly, listening to her friend, holding her crystal pendulum, which swung around in circles as if saying yes to everything her friend said.

"I think my family died here. I was a young man. There were seven of us. Other people in the village began to get sick and die. My mother, who was a kindly soul, took food and milk to them. I think she was the one who brought the sickness into our family".

Anne just nodded and quietly said, "Go on".

"One by one my family became ill. The monks took them into what we now know was the plague house. A sort of hospital. Recently I had another vision. I saw the monks emerging from the field. There were fewer now as some of them had died. They appeared to walk straight through the farm buildings we have now. I followed them – although they told me not to. When we reached the building which I can now see clearly. It looked more like a barn and probably was in those days. People were lying on the floor crying out. Calling for water and help. The monks did what they could. I helped them as best I could. There was little we could do except drag the bodies to the open area which I now know was that corner we went to".

Maggie paused again. Her face changing as she relived this experience. Anne quietly got up and fetched a glass of water for her friend. Maggie gratefully sipped from it. Then she was ready to continue.

"I caught it – the plague".

Anne asked how she knew. It began with a fever and swelling under my armpits. After a few days the swellings began to leak pus. I was vomiting. At first the monks let me stay with them – but it was too dangerous. My fingers were turning black and they said I would have to join the others in the hell hole of a barn. All around me I heard the moaning and crying out. People were left lying in their own vomit and excrement. At first, I was aware of what was happening, then mercifully I drifted into nothingness".

Maggie started to cry. She began sweating. Anne knew she had to bring her friend out of this soon.

"What happened then? Can you remember anything more?"

"Yes" replied Maggie, her voice cried out in anguish. "I heard my friends the monks say that there wasn't anything they could do. They had to save themselves. They boarded up the door, leaving us poor souls to die locked inside".

"And you were one of them?"

"Yes, I was left to die".

"I think you have gone through enough Maggie. I want you to come back to now. I believe this is why I felt so much torment still coming from the earth under our feet. I was getting horror and pain and great sickness. I will go back now to that area in the field to try to put them at rest and release them from their terrible deaths. They are still trapped and you were one of them".

Anne spent well over an hour in the field. She explained that she couldn't release everyone at the same time. She had to work with each one separately and that was why it took so long. Each one had to be sent to the 'light'.

"It's clear now. I sent your soul in that life back to the other side. I think your monks will have also gone. They have no need to look after the poor folk who died in terrible circumstances. I also lifted the energy from the corner of the field. I think that animals will begin to graze there and if anyone dug down several feet, they would only find a mass of skeletal bones. Oh, and by the way I think the church up on the hill was burnt down the same time the monks dwelling was".

"Thank you, Anne. I am feeling as though a terrible cloud has lifted".

"It has. Just get on with your life. There is nothing here anymore. Just a hollow in the field, and if anyone cared to dig where I marked the monk's field, they would probably find old stone walls and maybe an oak beam or two. Nothing else".

BLIND DATE

I had arranged to meet my date at the pub nearby. I knew the place. It had an arboretum next to it which I had always wanted to explore. I arrived early to give myself time to wander through the wood, filled with some magnificent ancient trees, some of which had been there hundreds of years, perhaps dating back to Henry VIII's reign.

Bill Legh and I met on an online dating site. He looked nice. A warm smile and mousy coloured hair, combed neatly away from his forehead, and when we spoke to arrange the meeting, his voice was pleasant, not overbearing or dominant. Reminded me a bit of my father.

The day was warm and sunny. We could sit outside. A safe place to meet and talk and hopefully begin a new romance.

I had about 45 minutes to wait and so I parked my car and set off into the wood. The paths were winding, round the trees I thought. Under my feet soft, dry sandy earth marked out the path - kind to my summer sandals. A few other people with dogs said friendly hello's as we went in opposite directions.

It will be easy to wander back, I've only got to retrace my steps. I will allow myself twenty minutes of exploring. I didn't want to get back before Bill arrived. Somehow, I felt it might look as though I was too eager if I was waiting for him.

Suddenly I realised I had taken the wrong path. Instead of heading back towards the welcoming pub, I found myself going deeper into a tall pine forest. Where the hell was I? Immediately the place became darker and more foreboding. Trees stretched high into the sky. Few birds were chirping and going about their business of foraging for insects.

I decided to press on, hoping to wind back to where I wanted to be. The trees seemed taller and closer together. Their canopies merged up above, blotting out the sun. I glanced down at the path. No path! Where was it? How had I managed to lose the path? While I had been too busy thinking about my date and mentally falling in love with this unknown man, the path had just vanished. Just soft pine needles everywhere. Nothing giving me a clue as to where I was.

I looked down at my watch. Nothing there on my wrist! Had I forgotten to put it on this morning? I didn't remember knocking against anything to cause it to fall off. How long had I been out in this dark and now cold wood?

A crow squawked high above me in the treetops. My chest tightened with fear and I was afraid I was having a heart attack. Was it a crow – or something more sinister?

I forced myself to move forward. Was it forward or was I just going round in circles? I had no way of knowing. All the trees seemed alike.

A voice. Was that a voice I heard somewhere off to the right? No, I am not sure if it came from over there or elsewhere. The sound was comforting. Someone was looking for me. Then it became more menacing and harsher as though the person was getting annoyed when I didn't respond. I stopped instead of moving in the direction I thought the sound came from.

What did I know of this Bill? Almost nothing. We had talked – although he mainly asked me questions at the same time as telling me nothing about himself. Suddenly the voice reminded me of my father again. Not the warm friendly voice, but the other he used when he was really angry and caused people to back away.

Bill had been quite flirty on the phone, and if I am honest, just a little too suggestive. But I was ready to fall in love and had laughed.

Now I didn't know. What was he really like? The shout came again. Angrier I thought. I began to run – away from the voice. Faster. Stumbling over raised tree roots. Please God, show me the way out!

He was coming closer. In my panic I looked for somewhere to hide. I saw a large holly bush and decided to hide in there.

I didn't notice the sharp thorns tearing my hands and face, so desperate was I. Crawling under the branches, I half crouched and half lay against the trunk. He was coming closer. I could hear the sound of his feet as he scuffed his way through pine needles and dried leaves.

Oh God! He's got a torch! I curled up tighter dropping my head to conceal my face, but not before I realised it was the light on his phone. He accidently turned the light towards his face and I saw, not the kindly man on the dating site, but a face screwed up with anger. He called my name again and again. Each time harsher and more menacing.

I lay there not daring to move in case the rustle of leaves gave away my hiding place. My heart pounded. I was sure he must be able to hear it.

A sweep around with his phone torch and then he moved on.

I lay there for I don't know how long, bitterly regretting the lack of my watch – all the while thinking about him – about us. It was as if the last few weeks and months flashed through my mind.

A friend had signed me up for this dating site. I was quite inexperienced with that sort of thing. The man I had fallen for seemed nice and I'd felt comfortable.

Then I began to think back. At first, he'd seemed so normal, but not overly keen. That is until he began to ask me questions. In my enthusiasm to be open and honest, I'd talked about my very wealthy aunt who had left everything to me. House, money and all her worldly goods. I described the imposing Georgian farmhouse. The outbuildings and land. He asked me what I did for work and I, almost proudly, told him I didn't work, unless you counted the various charities. I told him about my financial guy, who had explained all about where my money was invested and what income I could expect. He asked me what sort of car I drove. Again, in a showing off kind of way, I explained that my aunt had an elderly Aston Martin, which for old time's sake, I was driving.

Later I realised he would have seen the distinctive car in the car park and had known I was already there.

I chatted on not realising that while I was opening up my life and my heart to him, he gave away nothing. Was his name really Bill Legh, or had he pinched it from the well-known local landowners? How old was he? He never said. It was only when I saw his face highlighted by the light on his phone that I realised he must have been much older than I'd thought. Had he displayed an old photograph of himself on the dating site? Was he married or had a family? Nothing. But the most sinister thing was what he wanted from me. Money? Was he one of those men who preyed on vulnerable women and scammed them out of millions? Would I have let him? Maybe.

They found me. Lying about ten yards away from the path. Unconscious. A large lump on my head. Had I bumped into a tree or was it something more sinister?

Afterwards all I could remember was the wood and how dark and scary it was.

I had no idea of how I came to be there. No memory of who found me lying in a heap with my clothes dirty and torn.

Nothing. Everything was obliterated from my mind.

TICK, TOCK, TICK, TOCK

Martha James had been looking forward to what she guessed would be her last visit to the old cottage formerly owned by her grandparents, both now deceased. It had been their home for over sixty years and now it belonged to her. Her grandfather died about eleven years ago and her grandmother five years later. It was because of this she was making her final pilgrimage.

She had flown home from Australia for her grandfather's funeral and that was the last time she had visited the pretty rose and wisteria covered house. She hadn't been around when the decision to deprive her beloved Granny of her home was made. Her step-mother wasn't quite so caring. The house had been left empty since the abrupt disruption of the old lady's life because she was adamant she might want to move back and live in it. She never got the chance. Since her grandmother's death almost two years ago, the house had been allowed to rot away.

Martha had driven over one hundred and fifty miles from her house near Bristol to meet the estate agent and finalise the sale of the house by auction.

She had so many wonderful memories of long summers staying there. With these in mind, she turned off the main road and headed along a narrow lane, smiling to herself. She left her car on the road to walk the hundred or so yards along the driveway.

As she walked Martha thought back to happier times. She'd

spent a lot of time with her grandparents. She particularly adored her grandfather, a lovely sensitive man with a love of all things to do with nature. It had been he who had taken the young Martha on walks and taught her the names of the plants and wild flowers. He was always quick to point out the birds who frequented their garden.

Her granny was a home maker. She excelled in what she called good straight cooking. Sunday roasts and apple pies were some of Martha's favourites. Granny was a fantastic seamstress and almost all of the quilts and curtains had been lovingly made by her. The house had always been bright and cheerful. She'd even made dresses for the little girl, and Martha's favourite, a cloth dolly, with a matching outfit.

It no longer looked the way it had been in her granddad's day. He was so meticulous about keeping his garden and grounds in pristine order. The grass was always neat and tidy with the edges trimmed. People said it could have been used as a croquet lawn it was so perfect

Her grandfather would have been in despair to see what it had become. Trees, which had always been cut back, now grew together over the drive making it feel like a dark tunnel and she hated it. To make it worse an ugly cloud slid over the sun causing the foreboding to build up in her mind.

She'd arranged to meet the man from the local estate agency. He was coming to take outside photos of the house to display in the catalogue for their next house auction. He'd said there was no point in having internal pictures as the house was in an awful state.

As she walked Martha thought back to happier times. She'd spent a lot of time with her grandparents. She particularly adored her grandfather, a lovely old man who stooped from spending so much time tending his garden.

Martha was dreading entering the house which had once been her second home and now was an almost derelict mess. She slowed her steps to delay the moment for unlocking the front door.

A bird suddenly flew straight out of the overgrown shrubs lining the unused path. Martha shuddered. Why was she so scared she mentally asked herself? She knew the answer, she felt someone was watching her from an upstairs window. Someone was willing her forward. The closer she got to the old house the more frightened she became. Snap out of it, Martha told herself. There was nothing to fear - but she was still afraid.

Reaching into her handbag she found the bunch of old-fashioned keys, one of which would open the front door.

A cheerful hello from the young photographer brought her senses back to normal.

"I'll just wander round the outside and through the garden and take the pictures I need. As soon as I have done, I'll get back to the office".

Martha heard herself say "Fine".

She really wanted to beg him to stay and explore the house with her. Sort yourself out, she murmured, you're a grown woman, have some sense!

She struggled with the heavy key. It didn't seem to want to go into the lock. With difficulty it turned and the door creaked open. The hall behind it smelt of mildew and dirt. She hadn't been in the house for a long time and she had never seen it like this before.

Martha stopped in the hallway and looked around at the mess. There was the old grandfather clock – her grandad's pride. She remembered sitting on the bottom step of the stairs every Sunday evening, counting the times he turned the key to wind it up for the week. It had made a rasping noise. One, two, three – up to ten. He would then check to see if it was the right time while she watched the pendulum swing sideways making a gentle tick tock noise. Her eyes filled with tears. The old clock face was covered in dirt and grime making it hard to see through the glass.

She called out, 'Granddad, I am so sorry! It is my fault it's like this. I was in Australia and too much involved with my job and life. I should have come back to look after the old place. I am so selfish.' Nobody answered her. Now she really did begin to cry.

She forced herself to go from room-to-room downstairs. It was hard to see much as the windows were almost covered with ivy and the encroaching bushes. A broken window pane had allowed the rain to enter and much of the old furniture had suffered. There were even signs a bird had fallen down the chimney and died in there. The curtains hung in shreds and what was left of handmade cushions seemed to have been homes for many mice. The hearthrug her granny had always been so proud of was full of holes.

Again, she had that eerie sense she wasn't alone. She pulled open the cupboard beside the fireplace where her grandmother kept her precious China and was met with a violent crash as shelves collapsed causing cups, plates and her grandmother's special teapot to fall on to her feet. Martha leapt back with an anguished cry, followed by sadness in seeing these beautiful things her grandmother had treasured destroyed in a second. She called out again to her grandfather, long deceased.

"Granddad, where are you? I need you". Again, she felt the presence of someone beside her. Was it good or evil? She couldn't tell. Was that a movement in the corner of the room? Was someone hiding there ready to leap out at her? Then she smelt it – the pipe tobacco he'd always used. Surely, he'd had his chair in that corner? The scent of it was so strong she knew it was him.

Martha forced herself to visit the kitchen. It was just the same.

Granddad had offered to put in a new modern kitchen but granny always said she was happy with what she'd got.

Looking around she knew her step-mother had made no effort to move the old lady with any sort of compassion, or dignity. From the looks of it she had bundled a few clothes into a bag, put her in her car a driven away happy that she needn't take any more responsibility.

Martha couldn't bring herself to open cupboards. It was sufficient to see all the old pots and pans still carefully placed in their usual places. It was obvious a cat had been using the old cat flap. Martha hoped it had caught some of the mice inhabiting other parts of the house.

Martha took a deep breath and headed towards the stairs. She thought she was being followed. Was that an extra creak on the stairs behind her? My God, she told herself, I am getting paranoid!

Upstairs, if possible, it was worse. Never a lover of spiders, she ducked to avoid a number of large webs hanging from the beams at the top of the staircase. She shuddered as she thought how big the spiders must be to create the black masses in the corners.

She instinctively headed towards her old bedroom. Most of the loving things her grandparents had done to make her feel special were gone. Her bed was covered with the girly quilt her grandmother had creatively made, but it was now tattered and torn. Her books still on the shelf above the 'desk' her granddad had built were covered in damp and mildew – and then she turned towards the little chair and her cloth dolly. Dolly, she'd never had another name, was still sitting there. Martha reached out to pick her up and as she touched her, one green glass eye fell off and rolled towards the old iron fireplace and lay there looking at her. Where it had come from was now an eye socket with threads hanging down. Martha put a hand over her mouth to stop the scream coming out.

The sound of her footsteps seemed to have disturbed something behind the skirting boards. A steady gnawing sound began. Fear that whatever it was might break through caused Martha to step back in terror. At that moment something brushed her hair. A bat was flying around.

She couldn't take any more. She dashed for the stairs which would take her back down to the hall. Now hurrying and stumbling down the flight of steps she caught her heel in the ancient tatty carpet. It had been there as long as she could remember. As she tripped, she fell forwards trying to grab at the rails. Later when she looked back, she was relieved she had been near to the bottom. Suppose she had broken something – no-one would have known she was there.

Martha pulled herself up on the wooden bench oblivious to the dirt and dust. Then she heard it. The clock was being wound up. One, two, three, four, five rasping sounds, six, seven, eight, nine, ten – and then it stopped. She stared at the clock. It had been filthy when she entered the cottage. Now the face was shiny and clean and the time was perfect. As she looked at it the pendulum began to sway gently sideways and the gentle tick, tock, tick, tock began.

She ran out of the house, not caring she'd left it unlocked. She didn't stop running until she had safely locked herself inside her car. She hung on to the steering wheel with her head leaning on her hands while sobbing and taking huge gulps of breath to clear the taste and smell of the old rotting cottage.

This was the end; she later told the estate agent. Get what you can – I'll never go back.

THE SAND WORMS

Katherine had gone on holiday from England to visit some Australian cousins. It was her first visit and so she decided to take a coach trip to visit some other parts of this enormous country. Everybody was very friendly and made her feel welcome.

The tourist coach halted beside a vast still lake a few miles out from a homestead. Weed covered the shoreline area, some the colour of iridescent lime green, while a dull grey green weed further out spread over far more of the inland water surface.

The place where they stopped had a much thinner layer of the dark covering. A narrow band of lighter vegetation bridged the gap between the grassy bank and the clear water of the lake. The coach driver explained that the water was warm and fine to swim in. Passengers leapt off the bus and quickly put on their bathing costumes before charging towards the inviting prospect. Katherine held back because she had an intense dislike of sticky mud squelching up between her toes and the fear of what lurks in the mud made her heart turn over.

The other passengers jostled each other to get into the lake first, pushing through the responsive weed to reach the deeper water. Some swimming, some just wading, but calling out to the others to 'come on in' the water is great.

She shuddered as strange little pink and black wriggling creatures with many legs appeared from under the weed.

Katherine was the only one left on the soft turf bordering the immense span of still water, wondering why no ducks or birds were enjoying the natural area.

Soon everyone else was beyond the weed when suddenly the sandy bottom seemed to explode. Huge jets of water shot into the air. Enormous mouths, almost two feet across, of giant sand worms quite literally sucked my now screaming fellow travellers, inside their hideous, eyeless tubes.

For a moment she stood transfixed. Bile and vomit raced up her throat as she dropped down on to the short-tufted grass. Unable to move, she watched the sand calm down, motionless again beneath the reflective water mirroring the scurrying clouds.

Piles of discarded clothes surrounded Katherine as a sound brought her back to reason. She turned and saw the tourist coach, filled with all their possessions, disappear along the endless road.

CRASH

Hannah and her husband, Trevor, had bought this old cottage. It had been uninhabited for at least twenty, or more years and was in a poor state of repair. They were both fascinated with really old buildings and firmly believed in restoring rather than pulling down and building ugly modern monstrosities. There was a preservation order on the property, so they knew they had to be careful with what changes and alterations they made.

The couple had planned to do enough to make it liveable and then move in to complete the renovations. Ceilings were opened up to reveal ancient oak beams. Someone had said they were probably taken from sailing ships. As Trevor tapped on walls the wattle and daub could be heard falling inside. More work and maybe much larger costs to bring the experts in to help them. It wasn't the money – they'd plenty of that - but the time it would all take, and a longer stay in the rental home was more concerning.

Trevor spent time searching antique shops and fairs to find anything that fitted the time period of the original cottage, while Hannah carefully peeled back ancient layers of wallpapers to search for traces of the earliest decorations – and there were many.

They were finally able to move in. Hannah was very sensitive to energies and as long as they remained friendly, she was happy to let them remain. The couple had transformed the kitchen and one bedroom – theirs, and planned to spend most of their time between these two rooms.

In their exploration of the old stone floors, they noticed a change where it looked as though a doorway had been shut off. Curious to know why they began to investigate the wall alongside the huge stone flags. They needed to raise a couple of them and in doing so discovered another floor underneath. They still hadn't reached the base of the doorway and worked again to dig down further. This was the point archaeologists were called in. It seemed they had found something much older.

Having to be careful, they came across the bottom of an entrance which had been bricked in. Knocking away the bricks they found worn stone steps leading into what appeared to be a cellar with arched stone walls and low ceilings. Hannah was very frightened. Trevor and the one archaeologist on site with him quickly found torches and descended down into whatever they might find. A former coal hole with its rotten wooden hatch allowed narrow shafts of light to penetrate the cellar and cast shadows as the light outside changed. The garden was still completely overgrown and they hadn't noticed it. What they did see was obviously an entrance to another part of the cellars. The door was locked shut and looked as though it hadn't been opened for at least a hundred years. Trevor wanted to open it up immediately, saying it might have treasure hidden there, but Hannah insisted they left it sealed.

On a later visit to the hidden underground rooms, accompanied by one of the archaeologists, Hannah swore there had been noises coming through the walls. Trevor suggested it was just rats, but Hannah with her sensitivity to the occult knew she'd heard something like a child crying and feared a child had died and been locked away in there.

When they did eventually open the entrance, they all reeled back in terror. All three of them felt as if a powerful and evil spirit had been waiting for its chance to escape. Hannah cried out to the two men

45

ahead of her to watch out. She had a vision of a young girl. Clothes torn in shreds. Hair long and matted, and eyes so angry they made all three of them back away, cowering against the damp and slimy walls of the cellar. The girl's hands twisted and tipped with long nails shaped like talons came at them as though ready to gouge them.

"My God", whispered Trevor, "what the hell is that"?

By now Hannah was rushing back towards the stone staircase and the safety of the cottage. The two men not far behind. Slamming the door to the cellar they retreated to the kitchen.

"She was very evil. A young girl who'd had some sort of deformity or mental illness was shut in there to die". Hannah told them.

"How do you know? Asked the archaeologist.

"I just know. I can sense things. I think she was after me. It maybe she thought I was her mother. It was the anger and rage I could see in her face. It really terrifies me. She was very dirty and full of black evil. If she had got to one of us, she would have done some serious damage".

"Did she die in there"?

"Oh yes, she died but she doesn't know it. It will be very hard to convince her to go to the light".

"I didn't realise ghosts can hurt you," said the young man.

"Mostly they don't. But she would have left deep scratches and bite marks on us".

"What are we going to do?" asked Trevor.

"I think we will have to leave it for a few days before going back down there again. I saw signs of a much earlier building. Something that existed long before your cottage was built. Possibly going back to the Saxon period".

"I'm not coming!"

"You don't have to Hannah. I will get some advice on how to deal with this".

Trevor and Hannah were both very spooked by their encounter with the evil child and decided they needed a few days away from the evil permeating in the house, it was as if something had been let loose and it was going to be hard to contain it again.

Packing overnight bags and piling the dog into the car they headed for a hotel near Conwy. No B&B just rest. Their dog Freddie just loved running along the sandy beaches, chasing a ball until his owners became too bored or tired.

Unfortunately, they had to drag themselves back. Workmen would be arriving at about 8am on Monday morning.

Upon arriving back at the cottage, they unlocked the door with the only key they had. As the front door swung open, the stench hit them. Sewage, rotten apples and putrid flesh all seemed to flow at them at the same moment. Freddie turned around and leapt back into the car. He wasn't going anywhere, especially with a sensitive nose like his.

Trevor and Hannah forced themselves to enter. They made for the kitchen, the only place they really felt safe in. Trevor offered to take their bags upstairs, noticing on the way that the locked door to the cellar was open. What the hell, he thought. We had the only key – how could it be open?

Apart from that, and the dreadful smell, everything seemed normal – that was until he opened their bedroom door. A horrific scene met his eyes. He just stopped at the entrance. Hannah had followed him up. Instinctively he tried to hold her back. They both stood there and looked at the wreckage of their beautifully restored room. Except that it wasn't beautiful any more. The curtains looked as though they had been shredded. Bedding was torn and covered with filth that looked as though it had come from the cellar. The new carpet would never recover from whatever had been done to it.

Hannah gave a loud moan as she took in everything.

"Who – or – what could have done this"?

The delicate fabric of the silk curtains appeared to have been torn apart by someone using their fingernails. Pretty wallpaper chosen in keeping with the period, had been ripped from the walls and was hanging in long shreds. Drawers pulled out. Cushions and pillows lay in dirty heaps. Everything was a complete bombshell of a site.

Trevor caught Hannah before she fell. The shock showed in her face, and her body was limp. Half carrying her and half supporting her, he managed to get her back to the kitchen where he sat her down on the small sofa occupying the corner under the window.

"What are we going to do"?

"We have to stay here today. I'll get the builders to work outside. There's plenty for them to get on with".

It began to rain heavily. The sky becoming dark with wild black clouds obscuring the views across the fields. Wind noise increased and started to howl down the chimney in what would one day be their sitting room.

Suddenly there was an enormous 'crash'. Both Hannah and Trevor shook with terror. Without speaking, they each knew the other was saying – what the hell was that?

Trevor finally plucked up courage to go into the hall. At the bottom of the stairs and scattered around his feet was the remains of the magnificent chandelier that had been hanging from the high ceiling above him.

"Hannah, can you come out here"?

Reluctantly she made her way to stand beside him and look at the mess.

"What happened"?

"I guess the chandelier came loose from the ceiling and fell down".

"I don't understand. How could it have become loose? We know how carefully the electrician was in securing it to a large beam".

Trevor replied "I imagine he didn't secure it as well as he thought. We'll have to clear it up before someone, or one of the animals gets hurt by the debris. I'll go and bring the wheelbarrow and a shovel in. Please can you find a broom?"

Hannah looked as though she would have refused when Trevor said, "I can't do it on my own, it is too heavy. I'll need your help".

He wheeled the wheelbarrow in and they looked at the tangled mess. Parts of the old Victorian light fitting lay at their feet. Delicate arms which once held dozens of candle holders were now twisted and bent and beyond repair. The ornate original holders had long since been changed to electric fittings, but were now squashed and distorted chunks of metal and the most extraordinary sight, was not that the chandelier had fallen from the ceiling – part of the chain was still attached. The rest of it was among the heap of twisted metal and the broken glass of all the small bulbs which had been in the sockets on the hanging lights.

As they swept up the mess, Trevor pointed to a pile of filthy grey ragged clothes lying on the floor beneath the carnage.

"What is that?"

"It's her – or rather it was her. She's gone. We are safe now"

"No, we are not safe yet. We have one final ritual to perform. That bundle of clothes must be burnt. It is the only thing that holds her here."

This was when they heard the meow of a cat in the kitchen, asking to be fed.

"The cat is back. When she disappeared, we thought she'd found a new home, but she's back Trevor"

Freddie trotted in from the garden. It was at this time they both noticed the stinking smell had disappeared, leaving only the clean scent of fresh paint.

Trevor said, "Lets finish clearing this up. We'll start again tomorrow to complete the renovations".

Hannah repeated that they were now safe. All the negative energies had disappeared.

The old cottage had reclaimed itself back again.

I WANT A HOUSE WITH CHARACTER AND POSSIBLY A GHOST

Grace had always loved this part of Cornwall. She had enjoyed so many holidays staying in her Granny's cottage. She'd spent many childhood and young adult years here. Birthday parties and bar-be-cues and then the local discos were all part of her happy memories.

She was back staying in Cornwall with her husband Mark, their two boys and the dog called Blondie. They were in Plymouth having lunch before they went to the league football match between Plymouth Argyle and their home team. Mark had managed to get tickets for the three of them. They arranged for her to pick them up later so Grace had her freedom to visit old haunts. She loaded Blondie into the car and set off towards the tiny village where her granny had lived all her life.

Pulling up in front of the cottage, she was appalled at what she saw. The little white picket fence was gone, along with her granny's prized herbaceous borders. These had been replaced by ugly stone walls and a high ornate wrought iron gate, completely out of character with the rest of the village houses. None of the loving pretty plants her granny had grown for many years, now only landscaped shrubs, a garden designed by a professional gardener. Gone were the creepers which had sprawled over the front and roof. Gone were the old windows and the heavy solid oak Georgian door. All replaced with revolting PVC window frames and the old wooden door painted lilac! Then

Grace noticed the new porch on the front of the cottage, and if this wasn't bad enough it was flanked by fake Victorian carriage lamps. They are not locals, Grace fumed. They have got to be townies with appalling taste who bought the place as a holiday cottage.

She didn't stay long and wished she had never decided to visit her granny's lovely warm and traditional home.

Grace had always wanted to buy a house in Cornwall and she drove off to wander through the lanes, just looking, she thought to herself. She and Mark could live anywhere as they were both self-employed and didn't need a base.

I want a house with character and I don't mind if it has a friendly ghost, she told herself. Grace found herself at the top of a hill with views in every direction. She could even see the sea away to the north. She let the dog out for a few minutes while she breathed in the beautiful Cornish air.

She had looked everywhere for the right house, her dream home, and was beginning to think it didn't exist, when she went round a corner and there it was. Later, she asked herself, had it been an accident or had the house found her? Ahead of her was a tatty and tired Estate Agent's board leaning precariously against a stone wall, announcing that the 'imposing property with several acres' was For Sale.

The house itself was perched high up in the hills with extraordinary views. Windswept fields, dotted with sheep were between her and what looked like a farm away in the distance. Cloud shadows raced across the landscape and cast her into shade as she wrote down the name of a local agent.

Grace shivered for a moment, but felt drawn to the property with overgrown shrubs and grass and ivy which obscured some of the windows.

Making her way to the nearby village she entered the doorway of the agent. She asked to see the house and explained she was here on holiday and that her husband and sons will need picking up from the football. The young man agreed to show her round straight away.

Dirt-streaked windows like enquiring eyes seemed to watch them as they approached the front door. Twisted chimneys, creeper clad, perched perilously on ancient tiled roofs.

The young man fumbling for the keys, jumped as a strand of ivy brushed his hair.

"Is it haunted?" asked Grace. The young man flinched but didn't reply.

Leaving Blondie, who didn't seem very keen to enter the house, in the car, Grace was ready to face whatever was concealed behind the imposing brick facade.

It is obvious the house has been empty for a long time. She led the way and was faced with a pyramid of sticks which half-filled the vaulted hall, dropped down the chimney by crow's hopeful of building nests high among the terracotta red brick chimney pots blackened by long gone fires. The Georgian front concealed an irregular sprawl at the back where generations of owners had added their tastes to the original Tudor farmhouse.

The young man opened the front door and ushered her in. She loved it at first sight. Rooms led off other rooms. Staircases seem to have built in a higgledy, piggledy way as the house grew wider and larger. High ceilings in the Georgian frontage gave way to low blackened ceilings of a more primitive period.

A twig appeared to move by itself. The young man stopped. She realised he was really uncomfortable. I'm sure it's haunted Grace murmured to herself.

She looked round the former drawing room and was sad to see the wallpaper stained with damp near the great open inglenook fireplace. Grace looked into the future and was already imagining what she would do. It would be wonderful for her family to be here at Christmas. A roaring log fire, decorated Christmas tree in the corner, large squashy sofas and the smell of mulled wine filled her senses.

The enthusiastic possible buyer wanted to see more and beckoned the young man to continue the viewing. He appeared to be reluctant as he hung back in the doorway. Grace went ahead of him leaving the newer part of the house to delve into the older passages and rooms. It was darker here because the windows with diamond shaped panes of glass were much smaller.

She moved steadily towards dark passages filled with un-swept cobwebs which hung like stalactites covered in dirt and grime. One caught her hair and now she shuddered. Suddenly Grace sensed an intense cold below her knees and felt afraid. A sound caught her ears and she turned to the thin young man to ask him what it was, only to find him speeding back towards the entrance.

She forced herself to go on looking – opening doors that led her to long neglected rooms with rubbish piles in every niche, left by old inhabitants of the long forlorn and forgotten place. Some of the rooms were completely empty as if the life had been taken away from them.

Something brushed her hair and she gave out a squeal of fright, but it was only a piece of loose wallpaper hanging away from the passage wall. She wondered whether to copy the estate agent and go back to the safer part of the curious house, but for some unknown reason she felt as if she was being drawn forward.

Pressing on and heading down dark and dirty passages where floor boards creaked under her feet, almost talking of friendlier days when people moved quietly about their work of dusting and polishing.

Grace thought she could still detect the faint sweet smell of beeswax drifting on the air.

One more door and then I'm done, she murmured to herself as she reached for the latch on a heavy oak door. The door swung open easily as though the hinges were well-oiled. A warm light emanated from the room – although no lights are burning. It is obviously a bedroom, but to her surprise there was no dust or dirt anywhere. The smell of beeswax was very strong and the chests and furniture appear to have been recently polished.

Grace looked around her, astonished by what she saw. Huge windows overlooking former gardens stretched along one wall. Sun shone into the room making it feel inviting. The walls were covered with hand stitched hangings and pictures, some of landscapes, and others portraits of family members.

Against one wall was a bed with hanging draperies. A little desk beneath a window. All seemed to be from another period. Dominating the wall above the fireplace was a picture of a very beautiful woman. As Grace looked at her, she got the feeling that the lady in the gilded frame appeared to smile and bid her welcome.

Grace knew she had been there before as she instinctively touched the unusual cross, she was wearing. Strangely it reminded her of the one the lady in the picture had round her neck.

Grace smiled back as she closed the door gently behind her before heading back along the dusty corridors to where the young man was anxiously waiting.

"I love it" she said. "But There is just one thing I would like to ask – why is one bedroom filled with lovely furniture, and the others left to rot in damp and mould? And who is the lady in the portrait?"

The young man looked at her as though she had truly gone mad and was a ghost herself.

"There are no rooms like that, they are all cold and dank and empty."

Grace smiled and said "I'd like to make an offer."

He looked incredulously at her. "Why would anyone want to buy a house like this?"

"I do", she said and taking out a bright red lipstick, wrote SOLD across the wooden sign. "I know it is haunted, but I am needed to restore it back to life."

Later when she took her husband Mark to see it, he was equally astonished, but he was used to Grace doing odd things and knew that when she had made her mind up, nothing was going to change it.

Grace led him towards the beautiful room, which she had already decided would be their bedroom. She opened the door and was surprised to find only another empty room. Nothing there.

She murmured to herself – the lady in the picture obviously wanted me to live here when she showed me the lovely furnished room. At that moment Grace decided to restore it exactly the way it was when she had seen it.

Over the years friends and family mentioned seeing a ghostly lady wearing a long dress gliding down the corridor towards Grace's bedroom. Nobody was frightened, just intrigued. Grace often whispered a thank you to the lady in the gilded frame for bringing her to this gracious house.

THE GHOST OF BROOK HOUSE FARM

It all began in 1992 in the old Cheshire, Georgian farmhouse we were living in. Our granddaughter and her mother were staying with us. One night at about nine thirty, Manon, the granddaughter woke up. She was nearly three at the time. We heard her crying and I went to see her to find out what was wrong.

Manon was sitting up in her bed saying she had seen a face. We couldn't console her so I took her downstairs. It must have taken an hour or so to persuade her to settle down again. At the time I put it down to the moon shining in through the window on to a mirror above her bed. But it couldn't have been that. It was a few days later, when thinking back, I remembered we'd had heavy rain that evening and everything was completely overcast and would have obscured the moon. Also, the window was too far away and too low for anything to shine on the mirror. We had a field and a steep slope in front of the house and unless the moon was actually at hedgerow level it could never have been reflecting off the mirror.

Manon settled down and we forgot about the incident – except we had no explanation for her behaviour.

It was perhaps about a year later when I woke up in the middle of the night and got a terrible shock. There was a man in our bedroom. I was glad that my husband was between me and the man. I remember thinking, what is he doing here? Was he going to murder us? How the hell did he get in? The house alarm was set and surely would have gone off. Then I realised I was looking at a ghost and stopped being frightened.

He appeared to be sitting beside the bed. His face was absolutely clear. As clear as seeing a real person in daylight. He had a very ruddy complexion with deep lines from beside his nose down to his mouth. He had, what I thought at the time, were steel grey eyes. He looked quite weather beaten, as though he spent a lot of time outside. It was as if his face was lit by candle light or one of the old paraffin lamps and he was watching over someone who was ill or dying. As soon as I realised, he was a ghost I stopped being frightened and was curious about what he was doing there in our bedroom. I remained completely still, watching him and wishing I could draw as I could have drawn his face. I lay there trying to mesmerise everything about him. I finally moved slightly to get a clearer picture. At that moment he literally began to fade away. He went from being so clear and very quickly became fainter. Within seconds he had disappeared and our bedroom was in total darkness. I lay there wondering who he was and why he was there.

Next morning I told my husband all about the experience but he had no explanation either. Over the next few days, I wondered how I could find out who he was so I wrote about the encounter and I submitted it to our local village magazine. On the day after the magazine was published four different older ladies phoned me. Each one of them said his name was Mr Bowler, it couldn't have been anyone else. He didn't have steel grey eyes, but bright blue ones with which he stared at people. The ladies all told me they had known him when they were children and all of them said they had been a little bit scared. Mr Bowler had been a farmer, which accounted for his complexion. One of them said she had ridden on his horse drawn wagon to the local railway station. Every day he used to take big steel churns of milk to be sent to Manchester to be processed. Don't think she could have been quite as frightened of him as the other three were. One of them asked me if he was wearing a hat. I had to admit I wasn't sure, but I think it might have been a battered trilby.

From then on, he became part of our lives. Manon was living with us permanently by this time. We weren't frightened as he seemed quite friendly – except my eldest son. On one occasion I put Simon into our spare bedroom, which was used by my husband as his study. Next morning I found Simon sleeping downstairs and when I questioned him, he answered that he couldn't sleep in that room because there was something scary about it. Don't think he ever set foot in that bedroom for the rest of the time we lived there.

Other odd things happened. We had a very heavy oak front door with a large iron doorknocker. It took some effort to get it to work. However, we regularly heard the knocker going and as there was no one there we put it down to Mr Bowler.

Another strange thing happened. My husband Michael had gone out. Manon and I were sitting in the kitchen when we both heard footsteps in the room above us – the one Michael used as his study.

Manon said, "I thought Gramps had gone out"

"He has" I told her.

"But I just heard him walking across the floor above us"

I'd heard it too.

Georgian farmhouses often have four rooms above each other, and our house followed this format. In the centre of the house was a wide hallway with stairs at the end. I went and locked the door between the dining room and the hall just in case someone had entered the house unbeknown by us. Then I went outside. Not a door or a window was open. There was nobody else in the house except Manon and me – and yet we both heard someone or something crossing the floor upstairs.

There were many other times when we were aware we were not alone, but, apart from Simon, none of us were frightened.

One day I was sitting having a mid-morning cup of coffee, on the patio area at the back of the farmhouse. As it had been a former farm, we had a large yard surrounded by four brick buildings, the house and three barns. It was into this yard a car appeared.

The man driving it asked me if the house had been on TV the night before. I was surprised, but said no it hadn't. He explained his mother had been watching television and had recognised the old house. I insisted I knew nothing about it. He went on to say that his mother, who'd been thirteen at the time, had been recovering from an illness when she stayed there with her uncle and Aunt Bowler. They'd had no children of their own. I remember blurting out – "He's, our ghost!"

We chatted for a while and I invited him to bring his mother to visit. A few weeks later he phoned and told me his mother was visiting and he added he hadn't told her anything, but just suggested she might like to see the old house again.

They arrived and I asked her if she would like a tour of the farmhouse before we had coffee. Downstairs had changed quite a bit. Our dining room had once been the original kitchen. You could even see where the former back door had been. Our kitchen had housed the big milk churns Mr Bowler used for delivering milk by train to the city. Our big sitting room had once been two smaller rooms. One for the family and the other was especially for guests – the parlour!

Upstairs we headed into Michael's study. The room where Manon and I had heard the ghostly footsteps and where my son had refused to sleep.

The old lady immediately said, "I remember this room. This is where my aunt kept her jars of homemade jam and chutney."

60

We crossed over the upstairs hall into my granddaughter's room and the old lady said it had been hers.

The most interesting bit was when we went into our bedroom where the ghost of Mr Bowler had visited us.

The old lady immediately said she remembered the room.

'It was my uncle and aunt's bedroom. There was a little round table over in that corner' she said as she pointed to the corner. 'My uncle kept all of his medications there. He suffered from arthritis, you know – and he had a chair beside the table'.

My jaw dropped. That was exactly where he was sitting when I saw him.

Perhaps the most curious thing was that he hadn't died in the old farmhouse, but had moved at least twice before he'd died.

The other strange thing was that the old lady had brought a photograph of Mr Bowler, his wife and his Collie dog. Mr Bowler was wearing a sort of trilby hat!

THE OLD MAN WHO HATED YOUNG GIRLS

The two old friends settled themselves comfortably at a table outside their local pub, each with a pint of beer at their elbows and old-fashioned baskets at their feet laden with vegetables newly dug from their allotments. These they would take home shortly for their wives to prepare for dinner. They were both tired from the digging and weeding their vegetable and fruit beds.

They were watching a large furniture van being unloaded with a new family's worldly goods.

"How long do you reckon they'll be here?"

"No idea. Nobody stays long. It's the cottage, you see. It doesn't keep people for long".

"Why is that?"

"It's an old story. My granny used to talk about it. She's long gone and so is the old man who lived there – and is still said to haunt it. In her time, it was two attached small cottages. Now it is just one house. Hasn't changed much. Nobody stays long enough to do a lot".

"I'd forgotten your family have lived in the village for a long time".

"Back to the Doomsday Book it is rumoured".

"I've been here seventy years – but am still made to feel like a newcomer".

"I remember you from our first day in school – it's a long time ago".

Both men took a large gulp from their pint-pot.

"Go on about your granny and the old man".

"The old man lived in one of the two cottages. In those days it was just one room downstairs where all the cooking, living and eating took place. Outside was the old 'privvy' – probably an earth closet in those days. I think the little shed is still there – at least it was when I last had a look round. There was one bedroom above the living area. The whole family packed into the two rooms. I believe they had five kids. Don't know how they coped".

"Go on, Jim. I want to hear about the ghost".

"The story my old granny used to tell was that the wife died leaving him with the children. Died in child birth and taking the child with her. Well, the old man, he wasn't that old then, decided to ask a young girl to marry him. She quite rightly thought it was to look after his kids. Probably correct. She told him no. She was known in the village for being a flighty bit. Anyway, she said no and the next thing was she went to work as a maid in the manor house in the village. Some handsome young men servants there, it was said. Thought she could do better than an old man with five kids".

"What happened then"?

"Well, so the story goes, he turned against her. Began shouting 'hussy' at her when he saw her around. He never did marry again. Turned against young women – including his three daughters. They couldn't wait to get married and move away. He began calling them hussies as well. The two sons went off. One became a gardener at the manor house and the other moved to London, it was said. You know the woman Cath who lives in the village? He was her grandfather, I believe".

"What does she say about him?"

"Not a lot. Anyway, about fifty years ago the owners of the other cottage, turned the whole lot into one big cottage. That was when strange things began to happen. He's been dead about seventy years, I think. There was a big mirror on the wall above the old black cooking range in the old man's side of the cottages. It didn't matter what they did but every Thursday morning it had been taken off the wall and lent facing away against the side of the fireplace. They tried everything, including screwing it to the wall, but every Thursday there it was again. They said he didn't like mirrors. Maybe didn't like seeing his own face".

"That was weird".

"What was weirder was that they had to keep replacing the screws and things. Every week they disappeared. Literally just vanished".

The two old men finished off their pints, got to their feet to make their way home. As they passed the removal truck, the new owners came out of the house. The old men introduced themselves – Jim and Nick.

"Good to meet you", they said, while the newcomers told them they were Hugh and Rebecca – from down south.

"Our daughter, Mandy will be moving in with us shortly. She's fifteen. Staying with her grandparents for a week or so".

Jim and Nick looked at each other, knowing what the other was thinking – oh no, oh no, now the trouble will start! However, all they said was welcome to the village. Hoped they'd be very happy here.

All was peaceful in the cottage while the newcomers moved in and sorted out their things. Mandy joined them and although she said she loved her room, she didn't feel quite right about it – something was wrong, she told her mum.

About three weeks after Mandy had joined them, Rebecca, who was a bit psychic, thought she sensed a presence in what they called the little sitting room, formally the old living and kitchen area. This was in fact in the old man's part of the house.

She talked out loud, telling him he was welcome to stay. She wasn't frightened of him. She could have sworn later there was a sound like 'hussy'. Rebecca immediately felt cold and shaky. She shuddered and imagined something or somebody was saying – "How dared she say he could stay in his own home".

This was the day it all began.

Mandy had joined the local tennis club and was out for the evening. Saying goodnight to her parents, she took herself off to bed, followed by their dog. Nobody knew what kind of dog she was – a mixture obviously. Usually, Milly cheerfully followed Mandy into her room, but tonight it was different. The dog stood whimpering at the top of the stairs. Mandy tried to coax her in, but she wasn't going to be persuaded. Just then the door leading into the bedroom mysteriously slammed shut behind Mandy – shutting Milly out.

A little bit spooked, Mandy got ready for bed. She lay back and switched off the light. That was the moment the teenager felt that a terrible presence was shut in with her. Later when she told her mother she described it as if there was a vortex of evil energy spinning very fast at the foot of her bed. A feeling of terror swept over Mandy. Too frightened to get up and too frightened to scream, she lay there cowering beneath the bed clothes. It must have stopped because she had, much later, fallen asleep.

"Mum, something terrible happened last night", she said as she described her experience. Please can I change bedrooms? I can't sleep in there again".

Her mother believed her and said her daughter could move into the little spare bedroom. It wasn't nearly as nice but she could go there.

Later that day when Rebecca was sorting out the little bedroom another frightening thing happened. She was arranging a bedside lamp for her daughter when a sudden crash made her turn around quickly. A tall mirror, still unattached to a wall, had been leaning against it. As Rebecca turned, she saw the mirror lying smashed, face down, on the carpet across the room. There was nobody else in the house. Now Rebecca really began to feel afraid. Was it her fault? Had she un-leashed something terrifying? She sank down on top of the bed won-dering what on earth she could do. Certainly, she couldn't tell Mandy what had happened.

There were several bibles in the house so she moved one to each room and went round with a bundle of smoking sage, hoping these would help.

Things calmed down for a while. Milly, the dog refused to go upstairs. Things were moved around in the kitchen. Mugs and plates kept appearing in the wrong cupboards. A bowl full of roses she'd brought in from the garden were strangely lying on the floor with all the water tipped over them, although the bowl itself was exactly where she'd placed it. She accused her family of doing these things, but they had sworn they had nothing to do with any of them.

She and her husband decided to get someone from the church to come and exorcise the whole house, although Rebecca believed it was only the area where the old man had lived.

By now she knew about him. She'd talked to her neighbours,

and while they had been cagey, they did say there had been something wrong for a long time. One old crone who was known to be a bit senile even went as far as to ask her how long they expected to stay.

Rebecca replied that they weren't going anywhere else. They loved the cottage and the village. The old lady almost cackled as she said, "You'll be moving on. Everybody does. He won't let you stay. He'll see you off like he does to everyone. Nobody can take it. You'll go, you listen to me. He will see you off, same as he has everyone else. And you've got that young girl living there. He hates young girls ever since that maid turned him down. He will soon start saying she's a hussy just like he did to her".

Rebecca then remembered believing she'd heard someone calling her a hussy just after she had told him he could stay.

One evening, before the vicar could come to clear the house of negative spirits, the three of them were sitting in the little sitting room when they all heard heavy footsteps above them in what had been Mandy's bedroom before she moved into the spare room. Mandy cowered in her chair.

"Mum, there's a burglar up there!"

Hugh, who wasn't admitting he was scared, agreed to go and have a look. Carrying a long handled wooden post, he'd brought in from the garden, he crept as quietly as possible up the stairs. Rebecca and Mandy heard him walking around and hoped the burglar wouldn't attack him.

When Hugh reappeared, he was shaking his head.

"There was nobody up there. The weird thing was that every cupboard and drawer was open and all the things were scattered all over the room – as if someone had been looking for something. Neither of the windows were open, and the door into the bedroom was

67

closed. Nobody could have come down the stairs because we would have heard them".

Rebecca just whispered, "It's the ghost of the old man".

Just then a wood pigeon clattered into the window.

"I think the old woman was right. We are leaving as soon as we can".

"The man from the church is coming in a few days", said Hugh, "let's give him a chance".

A few days later, Mandy was staying over with a friend while Hugh and Rebecca went to a dinner at the golf club. They'd had a lovely evening and Rebecca was preparing for bed. Hugh wanted to catch up on some golf on TV.

She sat on her stool in front of her dressing table and mirror and began taking off her make-up. As she sat there staring into the mirror she watched in horror as her face changed in front of her. What had been a pretty forty-five-year-old face began to age, gradually becoming older and uglier. Her hair became long and grey and straggly. Her mouth turned down. Wrinkles and lines crisscrossed the image. The ghastly old woman who looked like a witch was gradually turning into an old evil man. As his wretched face looked out of the mirror and he grinned. An almost toothless twisted smile greeted her with a knowing look. She was about to scream when she saw an invisible hand writing in red across the face of the mirror – 'hussy'. Now too frightened to let any sound come out of her mouth she watched as the glass in the mirror cracked and broke into a hundred pieces.

Now she screamed and Hugh dashed upstairs. He found Rebecca sobbing and surrounded by tiny pieces of glass – some covered in what looked like red lipstick.

"What happened"?

Rebecca could barely speak. She just pointed at the mess of glass.

"It was him! He wants us out! He told me early on, soon after we moved in – 'how dared I tell him he could stay in his own home'. And he called me a hussy". That's what he wrote on the mirror – hussy".

"Come on downstairs. I'll pour you a large brandy. And by the way there was a message from the church minister. He's coming tomorrow morning. If he can he will send the old man away. He told me that the ghost was probably trapped on earth and needed to be sent to the light. He sounded convincing. I believe we will be safe in future, but for tonight, while you finish your brandy, I'm going to phone the hotel just down the road and book us and the dog in there. We'll get back in good time for the minister – and I think we'll just leave the broken mirror so that he will be able to see what he is up against".

THE ANCIENT PRIORY
The year 1955

The young man smiled to himself as he drove his own, albeit rather battered car, to meet possible buyers for the old building. He had only recently passed his test and he felt very proud of the old 'banger' as his rugby playing friends rudely called it. He laughed as he headed towards the ancient priory somewhere in Wiltshire. He dreamed of selling it and buying drinks for all his friends in his local pub.

The priory had originally been built in the 15th century and had housed Augustine monks who made themselves wealthy at the expense of the local villagers. They ate well and drank well and lived in a fine building, while the villagers suffered from land seizures by these so-called Holy men.

When Henry 8th declared himself head of the Church in 1536 and ransacked every monastery and nunnery in the land, the monks had suffered. Many had died when their fine buildings had been burnt down and others of starvation. None of the villagers made any attempt to assist them. Memories were too long.

Tony was only just seventeen when he joined a local firm of estate agents. He was really chuffed the bosses were entrusting him with the possible sale of such a large house, which had been converted in 1587 into a private dwelling. The house had been passed down through the generations and was now owned by a distant relative who lived in Australia. The man had only once visited his inheritance and

70

decided it was far too much of him to take on the restoration of the ancient, tired building. So, without too much hesitation, he'd put the house on the market.

Tony had only been allowed to show a few tiny cottages or terraced houses so far. He was excited his bosses thought so much of him they were trusting him with such an important sale. His senior partners were quietly smiling to themselves. This might sort out the young man who was rather too full of himself. The building had some terrifying tales of dark and frightening events – and, besides, none of the others had wanted to visit it. Let Tony go they agreed. Most of them secretly hoping he would have a scary experience.

The young man drove through winding lanes and over down-land and rolling hills to reach the property. He arrived first and was a bit daunted to find he couldn't drive up to the front of the house because the main gate into the open parkland surrounding the house was rusted and locked shut with a large chain and padlock. However, a small side gate allowed him access. He stopped his car and left it facing the gates and sat there waiting for his clients to arrive. He couldn't wait to tell his mates about it at the pub that night!

After about half an hour later the husband and wife turned up. They'd got lost they said. Tony was not surprised. The husband carefully turned their car around to face the direction for their next stop.

They passed through the narrow entrance into the untidy grassy area. Tony and the married couple strolled up towards the front door. Tony had been told not to bother trying to open it as it hadn't been opened for years. As he led them towards the side entrance a flock of crows swept out of the surrounding trees and swooped down towards them. Not sure if they were merely surprised to see people, or whether they were in fact menacing, the three of them quickly entered the house. It was quite dark inside but not dark enough for them to feel uncomfortable. Tony instinctively pressed the light switch. Nothing happened of course because the electricity had been off for many years.

They made their way along a panelled passage where it was obvious the woodworm had enjoyed house room for a long time. By now all three of them were beginning to feel anxious. The wife, Jane, got between Tony and her husband, whose arm she clung on to.

"I don't like it here, Geoffrey" she whispered to him.

"We are here now, so we might as well see the rest of the house" replied her husband.

They entered what would have been the main hall. High mullioned windows gave light into the room, but also created shadows, some of which appeared to move. Jane gave a little shriek when a piece of the ancient panelling crashed down from high up on the wall to almost hit their feet.

Tony, who was equally fearful, decided he had to go on with the viewing. He talked loudly about the antiquity of the building, its history and of the families who'd lived there over the centuries.

They all heard a dog barking somewhere. Tony was surprised as he understood the place was completely empty.

As Jane and Tony passed through the hall, they both cried out at the same moment – "Did you see that?" Geoffrey quickly turned towards the direction they were looking. He caught a glimpse of an old brass fireguard gently rocking backwards and forwards in front of a massive empty fireplace, big enough to have roasted a whole ox.

"Who did that?" Jane whispered.

"It was probably just a gust of wind", replied her husband, but they knew it couldn't have been. Tony had heard rumours about the old house and its ghosts, but he had always dismissed them as fairy tales. Now he wasn't so sure. Maybe it had once an open space without the guard and the unseen servant had pushed against the heavy free standing brass fire screen. He couldn't think of any other explanation.

But there was nobody there and he didn't say anything.

Really frightened now, they moved into the next room. Floorboards creaked as they walked. A faraway door slammed shut above their heads. Unexplained noises seemed to increase.

Tony opened another closed door and was surprised to see what had obviously been the family chapel. What appeared to be an altar with a large cross greeted the three of them as they stepped through the old ornately carved door. He was surprised that nobody in the office had mentioned the fact that house still retained the chapel. Was it his imagination or did he hear the sound of chanting? Shaking his head he began to think he was mad.

Jane began to whisper she'd seen monks walking through the stone cloister outside the chapel. Her husband suggested it was just old stone headstones in the ancient burial ground which looked like the hunched shoulders of cowled figures.

She could only say, "Headstones don't move, what I saw were monks walking one behind the other. She wasn't prepared to listen to reason. Tony had to agree, he was really spooked now.

Tony was just about to ask if they would like to see any more – downstairs or upstairs, when a sudden flash of lightening and a huge crack of thunder cut through the silence. Jane really screamed this time her fingers digging into Geoffrey's arm.

"Let's go! I can't stand anymore! Please Geoffrey lets go now – now!

In the instant flash of lightening, they had all seen a black menacing mass moving towards them. All three of them dashed to the entrance of the chapel. Geoffrey in his panic, while pulling Jane with him, almost slamming the door on Tony. Tony wrenched the door open and dragged it shut behind him. Now all of them were almost panting in their fear.

The three of them rushed back down the panelled corridor – Geoffrey knocking over an old bucket left behind by former servants. It clattered to the floor spilling the tatty mop across the stone flags, almost tripping Tony up. He swore but apologised quickly. Jane didn't even notice in her haste to leave the terrifying old house. Geoffrey was really worried about her. Her breath was coming in great gasps as though she was fighting to quell her terror. He wondered what he would do if she passed out. There was nobody around to help.

As quickly as they could they re-crossed the parkland to where the gate and their cars were parked. Geoffrey yanked open Jane's door and helped her stumble in where she slumped back against the seat, still in shock. He got behind the driving wheel and immediately locked the doors from inside as if to keep the evil spirits out.

Tony had to shout through the closed window, mouthing in parrot fashion whether they would like to see any more. As if in answer Geoffrey just drove away not looking back.

Tony returned to his car and climbed in. He too was sincerely shocked by the experiences. He needed to turn his car around for the drive back to the office, but he had to be careful as the turning area wasn't big and three-point turns were still fairly new to him.

Deep water filled streams lined the loose gravel drive. Stinging nettles and long thorny brambles crowded and almost covered the unkempt filthy drainage ditches. High overgrown spiky blackthorn hedges left dark shadows on the smelly slow running water.

Tony backed his car up but unfortunately one of his back wheels went just over the edge of the ditch. Swearing to himself, he got out to see how badly it was in. As he bent over something picked him up off the ground and threw him into the ditch. Fighting mad and ready to punch whoever had done this, he scrambled out of the muddy water. There was no-one on the drive so he rushed through the little gate into the parkland. No-one there and nowhere for anyone to hide. Not a bush or a tree – nothing. Then Tony realised that when he and the couple had walked over the loose gravel, their footsteps had made crunching sounds. Whatever had come up behind him had been absolutely silent!

Terrified that whatever it was must have been very strong to pick him up like that – he was a very fit rugby player. Tony jumped back into his car and drove himself out.

Back at the office the senior partner and his colleague looked at him. Clothes dirty and his face ashen. Something bad must have happened but they were not about to ask.

Tony said nothing to them, or to his rugby buddies that evening. One or two remarked it wasn't like him to be so quiet and subdued.

It was years before he began to tell people about his ordeal – and I understand he never went within ten miles of the ancient priory for the rest of his life.

SOME STATELY HOMES OF ENGLAND AND WHAT IS HIDDEN BEHIND THEIR DOORS.

These are a few ghost stories connected to stately homes. Apart from one of them when I did experience some odd feelings, the others have been related to me by people who were there. I have no reason to doubt these people and believe these sightings really did occur. I am withholding the names as I haven't got permission to use them. (The author).

THE HOUSE IN LANCASHIRE

I visited this large country house with a group of people from a club in the next village. There were about twenty of us. After having lunch in a local pub, we arrived for our afternoon tour.

As expected, this house was full of odd little rooms leading off dark passages with many staircases connecting parts of the house to others. We wandered up and down lots of steps as we progressed between different areas of the ancient house, where bits had been added on. We were shown the priest hole near an old well from which the household had drawn their water. I must admit just looking at the priest hole made me feel claustrophobic. It was so small and I felt scared when thinking about being shut in there while being hunted for by the anti-Catholics.

It was the little sitting room that made me uncomfortable. I felt as though some long ago woman fell or was pushed out of the window.

I asked, as I always do, if the house was haunted. The answer I got was curious. At the time we were standing in the great hall. A place where the lord and his lady entertained their guests. Looking up I saw a minstrel's gallery.

The guide began to tell us a story about this room. Apparently, a previous group were being shown around the house. One of the visitors, fairly disabled, decided she would allow the others to go on without her. She sat quietly on one of the chairs to wait. When the rest of her party returned, they apologised for taking so long and asked her if she was OK.

"Oh yes", she replied, "I wasn't bored. A little girl came in. She was dressed in a sort of fancy dress. Long and made of some sort of woollen fabric. She danced around and sang to me. She also chatted away – although I couldn't understand what she was saying because it sounded foreign to me".

The guide then explained that the woman had met and seen the little French girl from the 17th century. She often appeared to entertain visitors – but as in this case – she almost always performed when someone was on their own.

A LARGE HOUSE IN THE SOUTH OF ENGLAND.

My husband and I were staying locally and decided to visit this magnificent stately home. Still occupied by the same family – and still is. We joined a group to be taken around the house. At the end of the tour, I asked our guide if the place was haunted. Oh yes, she said. The present owners keep a 'ghost book' into which family, staff and visitors are encouraged to write down any experiences they'd had. I understood the current owner was looking for repeat appearances and dates.

I then asked this lady if she'd seen anything.

Her story was fascinating. She had been showing a group of visitors around. Rooms and furniture had red ropes across them to discourage visitors from entering or touching. Anyway, on this occasion the whole group had paused to look into the library. The guide said she felt very annoyed at seeing a young man sitting reading in one of the chairs. The lady guide made a note of it, planning to go back when her tour was complete to chastise this person.

A couple of rooms later, one of the tour groups pointed to a large portrait hanging on the wall and said, "Wasn't that the man we just saw in the library?"

It was. He was a member of the family who had been killed in the First World War. When the guide went back there was no sign of him – but everyone in the group of about twelve had seen him.

MY MOTHER WHO WAS STAYING AT A LARGE COUNTRY HOUSE IN SCOTLAND

This happened many years ago, probably in the twenties or early thirties. My mother was a guest in the house and the owner was expecting a large party. I think they were going to the Braemar Games. They would certainly be dining in the house, and probably attending a ball while staying there.

They were a bit short of staff and so mother offered to help out. She was given a pile of linen and asked to make up a couple of beds. As she was doing this, she realised she was getting invisible help. Someone was pulling up the sheets and tucking them in on the other side of the bed. A bit spooked she question the lady owner, who just laughed and told her an old housekeeper, long since dead, was known to help out at times like this!

A BEAUTIFUL ELIZABETHAN TIMBERED COUNTRY HOUSE IN CHESHIRE.

We had been loaned this house for a charity function I was involved with. I was helping with the catering that evening. With a few minutes to spare, I chatted to the caretaker and asked him if the house was haunted. I already knew other parts of the beautiful house were known to have 'friendly' spirits. What the caretaker told me was fascinating.

"You know where the cloakrooms are for hanging coats. It used to be where the kitchens were. They had a huge fireplace for roasting meat. Our flat is immediately above these rooms and our bathroom is over the roasting area. The kitchens were taken out, maybe forty (now seventy) years ago. But sometimes when we go into our bathroom, the smell of roasting meat is almost overwhelming".

A VERY HAUNTED HALL IN MANCHESTER.

It must have been twenty-five years ago this happened. At the time my friend told me the house was empty except for the odd piece of furniture. Sylvia (not her real name) and a friend of hers, offered to join the real Ghosts Busters to investigate the paranormal. She picked her friend up from a nearby village.

Odd things began to happen when they entered the Hall. Sylvia who was an excellent pianist sat down on a tatty stool in front of an old piano, but she felt as though she was pushed off. Someone else suddenly found they couldn't move their feet and saw a shadow across the floor where his feet were.

But the really weird things started when they had driven home. Sylvia's friend had to be dropped off. She told Sylvia she was really scared and asked her to walk around the outside of the house, which they did.

Sylvia watched her friend enter the house and began to move her car forward. As she did so the passenger door swung open. Muttering to herself and annoyed with the friend who obviously hadn't closed the door properly, Sylvia leaned across, slammed it shut, and gave it a couple of pushes to make sure it was shut. She moved the car forward to the end of the drive and stopped to make sure the road was clear. The passenger door opened again! Sylvia, now really frightened, grabbed a cross and a bible she had taken with her, while shouting at the ghost to get out, it wasn't going home with her. She grabbed the door handle and again slammed it shut and with more hysterical shouting, drove her car out and home.

ANOTHER STATELY HOME IN CHESHIRE

At the time when I was told this story, I was a training officer for a large Estate Agency firm. I trained almost all the staff, including the, mostly ladies, who did the accompanied viewings. We often talked how, when entering a property, you would get good or negative vibes.

One of my viewing ladies told me this story.

She was a volunteer at this magnificent house surrounded by its parkland. She was there working with the flower arrangements. She said that in one of the first rooms visitors could enter, there was a round table and she was tidying up the flower display.

Someone behind her began screaming and saying she'd seen people being hung. The poor woman was in such a state she was taken into one of the private rooms. The woman kept on crying, now whispering, that she had watched people being hung. When she was able to, she was taken home by friends, who had witnessed her outburst.

Everybody was stunned by what had happened. Nobody could work out what she'd been saying – that is until, quite a long time later, when it was discovered that the part of the hall, she was in had once been an area where people were hung, drawn and quartered!

THE FINAL JOURNEY

I knew what it was like to be out of body. The first time it happened unexpectedly. I was lying on my back on my bed in California, my hands behind my head and my ankles crossed, just relaxing and trying to get rid of the negative things going through my mind. I was in a dark place, upsets in my marriage, not knowing where to take my life – and then suddenly it felt as though hundreds of thousands of electric volts were pulsating and entering through my ankles. I couldn't move. It was as though huge pressure in my back was pushing me off the bed and up into the room.

I was surrounded by the most incredible golden light and I realised I didn't have to breathe – I was just existing. The peace and happiness were overwhelming. If this was death, I was happy to go forward. I didn't want to get back into my body. I looked down on myself lying there so peacefully. With a slight movement I was hovering over the school next door, watching the children playing in the yard. Next thing I knew I was back on my bed. After that it was easy to get out of body and to experience it again and again.

So, dying was just a further happening I was expecting it because I had known for some time that the end – or rather – the beginning was coming nearer. The feeling of peace was overwhelming. The lightness in my body exceeded anything I had ever known. I was on my final journey.

There were the tunnel people talked about – but it was more like a strip of light, getting brighter as I progressed through this magical place. I could see shadows against the golden glow. These were family and friends coming to meet me and to show me the ropes. You are never allowed to go to the other side on your own because it could be frightening. Gradually they became clearer. There was my mother and slightly behind her, my father. Other people crowded towards me. I couldn't remember who some of them were, but I guessed we had known or been part of each other's lives over a thousand years or more. I did recognise my servant from Egyptian days holding a dog on a beautiful lead. My dog from that period and the one I had just left. I recognised her because I had always thought she looked like Anubis, the jackal God of the underworld. Her big ears, sticking up sharply on her head and the long-pointed nose were identical to the creature I had walked in the beautiful city on the edge of the river Nile, as we now call it.

Although I was surrounded, nobody touched me. I was as yet unclean. All their robes were almost dazzlingly white, while mine a dull almost grey colour. I learnt later that they were dressed like this for this momentous welcoming ceremony. At all other times people wore the richest and brightest colours of every type of style. They led me to the Temple of Remembrance and Sorrow. A place everyone must visit as soon as they reach the other side. I knew what was coming and was fearful. I had to face my past life and see and feel the hurt I had done to everyone while still on Earth. There in front of me was a huge screen, much like a big modern television I had left behind. Gradually people passed across the screen which was encased in a sort of table. Although there was no sound, I could 'hear' what had been said or done. The agony of seeing myself behaving in such ways, towards people I loved, and yet let down, made me want to drop down on to my knees and beg for forgiveness. But somehow I knew I was receiving their understanding and that they were forgiving me. But of course, they understood and were forgiving, they'd all been there themselves – some of them like myself many times. I don't know how long I was in this room of sorrows. It seemed like a whole lifetime but it was probably only a matter of Earthly seconds.

It was over and I was ready to meet my family and friends. As the door swung open, I realised my robe was as white and dazzling as all of theirs. They looked younger than I last remembered them and completely free of any disabilities they had suffered on Earth. We had a wonderful party, nothing like that on Earth – no food or drink, but more a meeting of joyous minds.

I wandered through amazing gardens, full of beautifully scented roses and glorious climbing shrubs. All my former animals gambled along with me. Glad that at long last I had come home.

Later I would visit other temples, some dedicated to music or literature, some to learning and one where I would meet up with my own spirit guides to discuss what I had achieved and learnt in the latest lifetime and whether I needed to return to experience more Earth lessons – but that would be my choice when, and if I decided to return. How many more lives would it take to reach the level of wisdom where I could teach others – perhaps as a spirit guide? These guides have lived on Earth and understand – not Angels who have never lived as we live, but our guides have been through everything we have done and know our strengths and weaknesses. Right now, I never want to go back again. The lessons get harder and tougher.

Milton Keynes UK
Ingram Content Group UK Ltd.
UKHW051439050724
445183UK00009B/14